Number Activities

Ray Gibson

Designed and illustrated by Amanda Barlow

Edited by Fiona Watt and Jenny Tyler

Contents

First published in 1999 by Usborne Publishing Ltd,
83-85 Saffron Hill, London EC1N 8RT, England.
www.usborne.com Copyright © 1999 Usborne Publishing Ltd.
The name Usborne and the device ♀ are Trade Marks of
Usborne Publishing Ltd. All rights reserved. No part of this
publication may be reproduced, stored in a retrieval system,
or transmitted in any form or by any means, electronic,
mechanical, photocopy, recording or otherwise without prior
permission of the publisher. FIrst published in America1999. UE
Printed in Portugal.

I can count

Contents

I can count

Follow the instructions in this part of the book to print fun pictures, each based on a different number. Most of the printing is done with potatoes cut in half and your fingers. You will need a paintbrush to finish off some of the pictures.

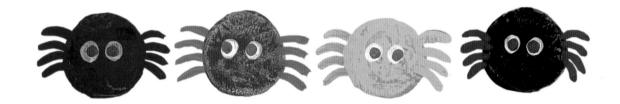

Perhaps you can think of other things to print or paint for each number too.

Opposite you can see some tips on potato printing. You will need a big potato and a small one. Ask an adult to cut them for you. You can keep your potatoes in the refrigerator for a few days. Wash, dry and wrap them up first.

If you don't want to get your paints out, you can use the pictures for counting practice.

Potato printing

1. Lay some kitchen paper towels onto a thick pile of newspaper.

2. Pour paint on top. Spread out with the back of a spoon.

3. Cut a potato in half. If you like you can make a handle by cutting it like this:

4. Lay your printing paper onto another pile of newspaper.

5. Press the potato in the paint. Then press it onto the printing paper.

6. You can print two or three times before putting more paint on.

I can count to 1

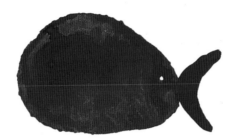
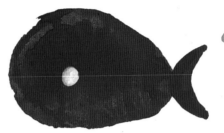

1. Print a body with a big potato.

2. Add a tail with a brush.

3. Finger paint a white eye.

4. When dry, add a black middle to the eye.

5. Paint a big mouth with a brush.

6. Finger paint a waterspout.

1 whale

I can count to 2

1. Print a black body with a big potato. Leave to dry.

2. Print a white tummy with a smaller potato.

3. Add a yellow beak with a brush.

4. Paint 2 black flippers.

5. Paint 2 orange feet.

6. Paint a white and black eye.

2 penguins

I can count to 3

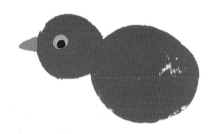

1. Print a body with a big potato.

2. Print a head with a small potato.

3. Paint a beak and an eye.

4. Paint 3 head feathers and 3 tail feathers.

5. Paint some legs with a brush.

6. Add 3 toes to each leg.

3 birds

I can count to 4

1. Print a body. Print eyes on top with your finger.

2. Paint **4** legs with a brush.

3. Paint some toes on each leg.

4. Print white spots in the eyes with your finger.

5. Print black dots in the eyes. Paint a mouth with a brush.

6. Use your finger to print **4** spots on the tummy.

4 frogs

I can count to 5

Flowers

1. Print a flower middle with your finger.

2. Print **5** petals with a small potato.

3. Paint a stalk with a brush.

Bees

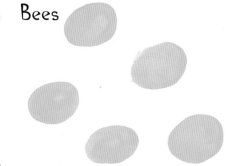

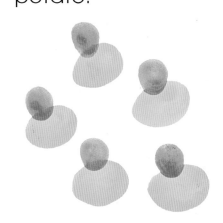

1. Print **5** bee bodies with your finger.

2. Finger paint wings on the bees.

3. Paint black stripes with a brush.

5 flowers

I can count to 6

1. Print a cat's face with a potato. Add ears with a finger or brush.

2. Print white eyes with dark dots. Use your finger.

3. Paint a black nose with a brush.

Mice

4. Add a mouth, and 6 whiskers.

1. Print 6 mice with your finger.

2. Finger paint an ear. Add tail, nose and eye.

6 cats

I can count to 7

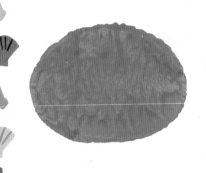

1. Print a body with a big potato.

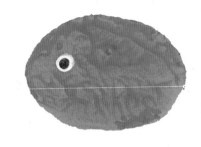

2. Print an eye with your finger.

3. Paint a tail and a fin with a brush.

4. Paint a mouth with a brush.

5. Paint **7** spines with a brush.

6. Print **7** spots with your finger.

7 fish

I can count to 8

1. Use a big potato to print a body.

2. Paint 2 stalks. Print eyes on top.

3. Print the middles with your finger.

4. Paint the mouth.

5. Paint 8 legs.

6. Put claws on the top legs.

8 crabs

I can count to 9

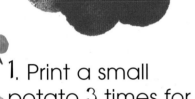

1. Print a small potato 3 times for a body.

2. Print a head. Finger paint a pointed tail.

3. Print eyes with your finger.

4. Print dots in the eyes. Paint a nose and a mouth.

5. Paint 9 legs. Put 3 on each part of the body.

6. Print 9 feet with your finger.

9 caterpillars

I can count to 10

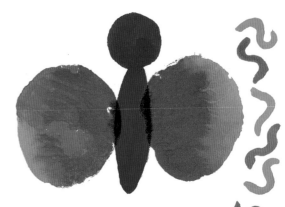

1. Print a head with your fingertip.

2. Paint a body with your finger.

3. Print wings with a potato.

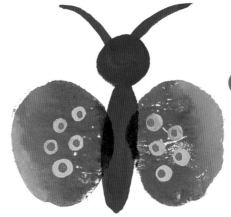

4. Paint 2 feelers with a brush.

5. Print 10 big spots with your finger - **5** on each wing.

6. Paint 10 dots inside the spots.

10 butterflies

I can count to 20

There are 20 ducks on these two pages. Can you count them all?

Now count how many ducks are swimming.

How many ducks have a yellow beak?

How many ducks have yellow feet?

How many ducks are pecking corn?

How many ducks have a worm?

24

See page 32 for how to paint ducks like these.

25

I can count to 30

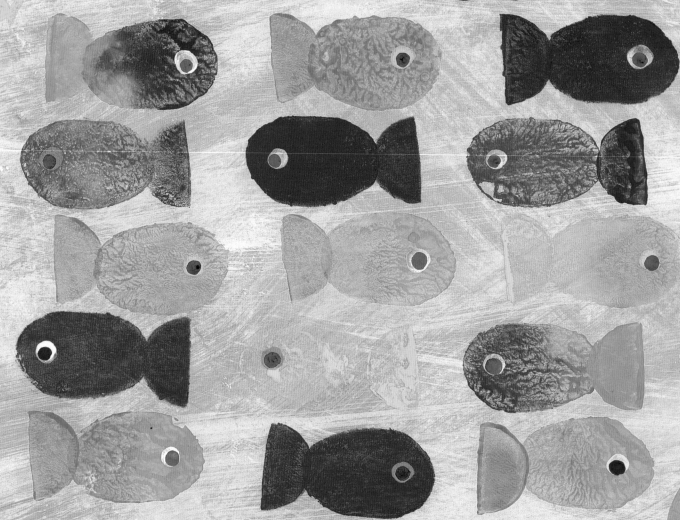

There are 30 fish on these two pages. Can you count them?

Now count how many of them have a green tail.

Find out how to print fish on page 32

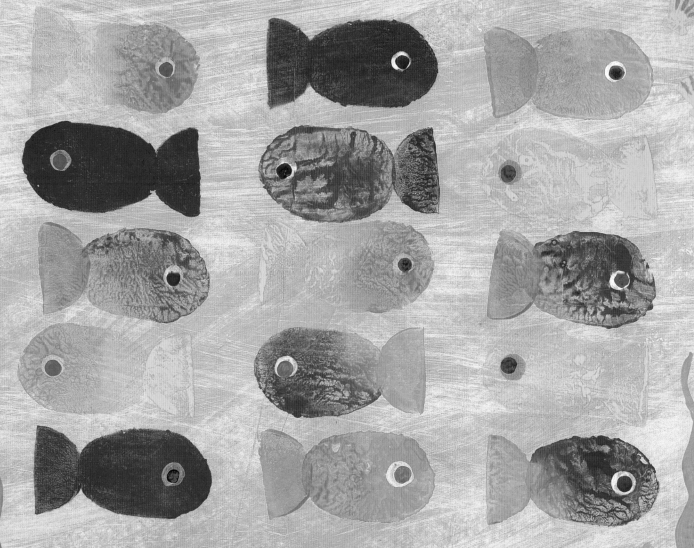

How many fish are swimming from left to right?
How many yellow fish are there?
How many fish have a yellow tail?

I can count to 40

There are 40 mice on these two pages. Can you count them?

Now count how many mice have a white tail.
How many pink mice are there?

Look back at page 14 to find out how to print mice.

How many mice have purple ears?
How many mice have pink ears?
How many mice have white ears?
How many mice have a piece of cheese?

I can count to 50

There are **50** spiders on these two pages. Can you count them all?

Now count how many black spiders there are.
How many spiders have pink legs?

Find out how to print spiders on page 32

How many spiders have green eyes?
How many spiders have black legs?
How many spiders are green with yellow legs?
How many yellow spiders are there?

Duck, fish and spider

For a duck

1. Print a body with a quarter of a potato.

2. Use a small potato to print a head.

3. Paint a beak and 2 feet.

4. Add an eye with your finger.

For a fish

 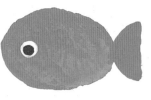

1. Print a body with a potato.

2. Print a tail with a quarter of a potato. Paint an eye.

For a spider

1. Print a body with a potato.

2. Paint 8 legs and 2 eyes.

I can add up

Contents

Adding

This part of the book is full of activities which ask you to cut things out and add them to the pictures. Sometimes, you will have to take things away and count again. Cut the things out quickly, but carefully. Don't worry about how neat they are.

When you start to add up, point to each thing as you count it and say the number. Later, when you are good at adding up, you may not need to point to things as you count.

You may find it easiest to start counting from the left side of a page and move to the right.

How many butterflies have spots?
Cut some spots for the others. Put them on.
How many butterflies have spots now?

Funny clowns

How many clowns
have hats?
Cut out hats for
the other clowns.
How many hats
are there now?

How many blocks have spots?
Cut spots for the rest.
How many spots are there now?

Mice and cheese

How many mice have a tail?
How many mice have no tail?

Cut a piece of yarn.
Give it to the mouse with no tail.
How many tails are there now?

How many plates have cheese?
How many empty plates are there?

Cut some yellow paper.
Put a piece on each empty plate.
How many pieces of cheese are there now?

Pretty princesses

How many princesses have crowns?
Cut out a paper crown. Give it to the princess without one.
How many crowns are there now?

How many rings have jewels? Cut out jewels for the rest.
How many jewels are there now?

Bears and bees

How many bears are awake?
Draw and cut out open eyes
for the others.
Put them on the sleeping
bears.
How many are
awake now?

2 honey pots have lids.
Cut out lids for the others.
How many lids are there now?

Count the bees on the
other page.
Add on the bees on this page.
How many bees altogether?

Caterpillar's shoes

Count the butterflies on this page.
Add on the ones on the other page.
How many altogether?

4 flowers have leaves.
Cut a leaf for the
other flower.
How many now?

How many shoes is the
caterpillar wearing?
How many legs have
no shoes?

Cut shoes from paper
and put them on his
legs.
How many shoes are
there now?

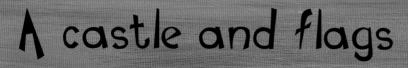 castle and flags

How many windows
are in the castle?
Cut 3 more from
paper and put them
on the castle.
How many windows
are there now?

How many flagpoles
have flags?
Cut out 2 more and
put them on empty
flagpoles.
How many flags are
there now?

How many rocks?
Add 1 more.
How many rocks
are there now?

Teeth and tentacles

How many teeth does the big fish have?
Give him **3** paper teeth.
How many teeth are
there now?

How many shells
have pearls inside?
Make foil pearls for the others.
How many pearls are there now?

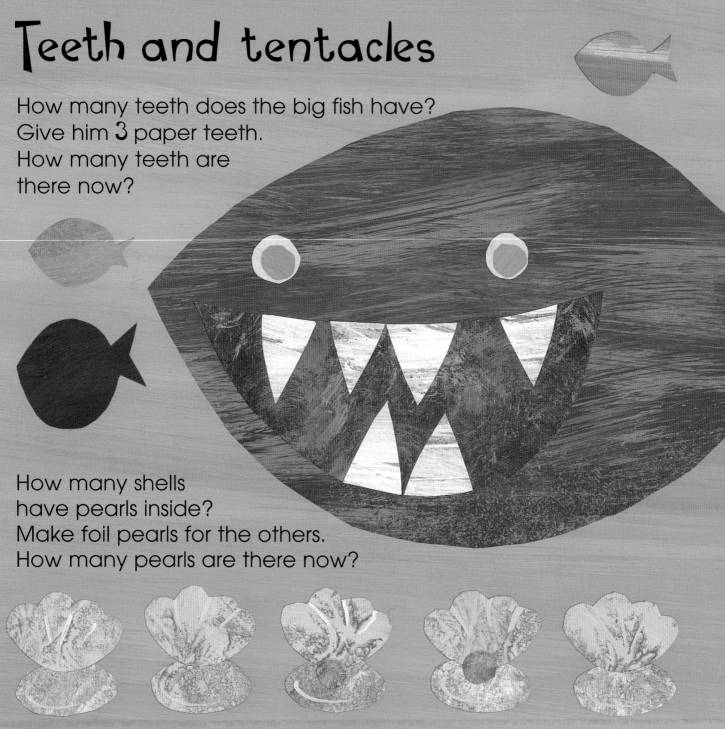

How many tentacles
does the octopus have?
Cut **2** more from yarn.
How many now?

Spotty animal

How many nests
have eggs?
Cut out **3** more eggs.
How many eggs are
there now?

How many spots does
this animal have?
Cut out **5** more spots.
Put them on the
animal.
How many spots
are there now?

51

Snowman

How many buttons does the
snowman have?
Cut **4** more from paper.
Put them on his tummy.
How many are there now?

How many birds
have a tail?
Cut paper tails for
the others.
How many tails are
there now?

Cut out **1** snowflake
from paper.
Add it to the others.
How many are there
altogether?

53

In the garden

How many flowers are on the bush?
Cut out **3** more flowers and
add them.
How many are there now?
Caterpillars eat **2** of the
flowers. Take them off.
How many flowers are left?

How many pots have a worm on top?
Cut more worms from yarn for the others.
How many worms are there now?

How many carrots
have leaves?
Cut out a paper leaf
for the one without.
How many carrots
have leaves now?

Penguin party

How many penguins have fish?
Cut out **6** more and give them to the penguins.
How many fish are there now?

Three penguins ate their fish.
Take **3** fish away.
How many fish are there now?

How many icebergs are in the sea?
Add **2** more.
How many are there now?

Hungry turtles

How many turtles have a
leaf to eat?
Cut out leaves and give
them to the others.
How many turtles are
eating now?

58

1 turtle finishes his leaf.
Take 1 leaf away.
How many leaves are left?

Wheels on the train

How many wheels does the train have?
Add buttons for the missing wheels.
How many wheels are there altogether?

How many parcels are in the wagons?
Add 3 more. How many now?
One parcel falls out. Take 1 away. How many are there now?

Jolly juggler

How many shapes
are balancing below?
Cut out **4** more and
put them on top.
How many are
there now?
3 shapes topple off.
Take **3** away.
How many are left?

Count the red
clubs. How many
are there?
Count the blue
ones. How many
altogether?

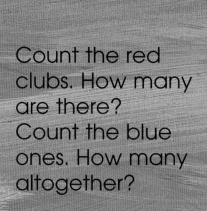

This juggler is juggling 3 things. Cut 3 more things from a magazine and put them on. How many is he juggling now?

The juggler drops 2 things. Take 2 of them away. How many things are there now?

Sheep in a field

How many sheep are in the field?
How many more do you
need to make **10**?
Use your fingers to
help you count.

How many more
flowers do you need
to make **10**?
How many more
birds will make **10**?

Fun with numbers

Contents

Number fun

This part of the book is full of different activities, such as the one below, which involve counting, adding, taking away or sharing. Some of the pages ask you to cut paper shapes to help you to count. You don't need to worry about how neat they are.

Going shopping

How many things are in this basket?

Cut pictures of any kind of food
from a magazine or newspaper.

Put the
pictures in
this empty
basket so
that both
baskets
contain the
same number
of things.

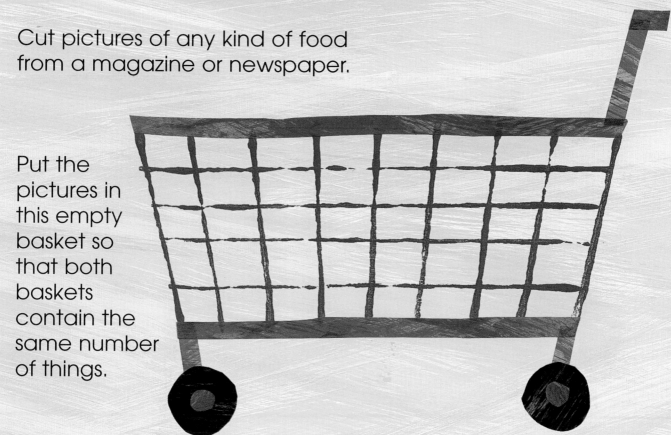

Sailing boats

How many boats are there altogether?

How many boats have **2** sails?

Cut sails from paper and put them on the boats so that each one has **2** sails.

How many sails are there now?

Spiders' Legs

How many spiders
are there
altogether?

How many legs
does each spider
have?

Which spider has
the most legs?

Cut some pieces
of yarn for legs.
Put them on the
spider so that each
one has 8 legs.

71

Busy cranes

How many boxes is each crane lifting?
How many boxes are the cranes
lifting altogether?

Cut some boxes from paper.
Add 1 box to each crane.
How many boxes are there
altogether now?

Add another box to
each crane.
How many boxes are
the cranes lifting now?

Planes

How many planes can you see?

Cut clouds from paper and cover 3 planes. How many planes can you see now?

Cover **2** more planes
with paper clouds.
How many planes
are left?

Shy monkeys

How many monkeys
are in the tree?

Cut big leaves from
paper and put them
over the small monkeys
to hide them.

How many monkeys
are left?

Hold up 1 finger for
each monkey that
is left.

One monkey goes
looking for food.
Put 1 finger down.
How many monkeys
are left now?

Builders' trucks

Cut out some bricks from paper. Put 3 bricks on the back of each truck.

Draw a circle with your finger around each group of 3 bricks.

How many groups of 3 are there?

Count all the
bricks. How many
bricks are there
altogether?

Now do the same
thing with 2 bricks
on each truck.

Greedy parrots

Use pieces of pasta as treats for the parrots.

Guess how many treats you will need, for each parrot to have 1 treat.
Give each parrot 1 treat to see if you were correct.

Give each parrot 2 treats.
How many treats are there altogether?

Give each parrot 3 treats.
How many are there now?

Roly-poly puppies

Cut **2** plastic straws into **12** pieces to make pretend bones.

Share the bones between the puppies until they have all been used up.

Share all the bones between **2** puppies. How many bones does each one have?

Try sharing all the bones between **3** puppies. How many does each one have now?

Four fat bears

Squeeze small
pieces of kitchen
foil to make **10** little
fish shapes.

Give each bear
2 fish.
How many fish are
left over?

How many bears
can have 3 fish
each?
How many fish are
left over?

How many bears
can have 4 fish
each?

Jumping frogs

Make a frog like this.

Fold some paper.

Make
two
snips.

Fold back the paper
between the snips.

Draw on a face and
some front legs.

Put your frog on
the big lily pad.

Make your frog jump on each
pink lily until it gets to the reeds.
How many jumps does it make?

How many jumps
does your frog make
if it goes on the
yellow lilies instead?

Spotted giraffes

Count the spots on the big giraffe. Then count the spots on the baby giraffe. Which has more spots?

Cut **5** spots from paper and put them on the baby. Which giraffe has more spots now? Which has the least spots?

Add a different
number of spots
to the baby.
Which has more
spots, now?

Party cakes

How many plates have **6** cakes on them?

Cut out shapes from paper to make cakes. Put them on the plates so that all the plates have **6** cakes.

How many cakes did you add to the white plate to make **6**?
How many did you add to the blue plate?
How many did you add to the yellow plate?

Something fishy

Cut small shapes from paper, about the size of the spots on the fish.

Cover each spot on the orange fish below, with a paper shape. How many shapes did you need?

Cover the spots on the other fish. How many shapes did you need each time?

Look at the
patterns of the
spots on the fish.

Make a pattern
with **4** paper
shapes on the fish
with no spots.

93

Busy bees

Draw **3** small bees and cut them out. Put **1** on each big flower.
Cut out **9** small squares.
Draw pink spots on **3** squares, blue spots on **3** and purple spots on **3**.

Put the squares into a bag, then pull one out. If it's pink, move the bee on the pink flower along one.
If it's purple, move the bee on the purple flower, and so on.

Put the square back into the bag. Have lots more turns.

Which bee reaches the
beehive first?
Which is second?
Which bee came third?

How many spots?

Count the spots in each picture.

Fold some kitchen foil around a piece
of cardboard, for a mirror. Stand
it along the straight edge
of each picture so you
can see its other half.
Count again. How
many spots does each
creature have now?